Savantia and Other Speculative Stories

A Collection of Short Stories

Volume IA

By Justin T. Cole

Cover Art: Astral Travel by Pavlo Kandyba
Cover Design: Michelle Kapschull

This volume is a collection of stories of various lengths, some of
which were originally posted on Reddit.

For any inquiries about representation, publishing additional
content, or other rights, contact

justintcole.books@gmail.com

Spare Time Books Publishing
PO Box 102
Buxton, ME 04093

Fonts used in this book:
        Trebuchet

Edited by G. Scott Swift

This book is dedicated to the many people who read the initial drafts of the stories contained within this volume.

Your encouragement and support have motivated me to use this as a stepping stone to what will be something much grander.

Special thanks to my parents for making this book, and any that come after, happen.

Edition Note:

This is the first half of
Volume I.

The overall volume was broken in twain to make this book an easier format for portability and on-the-go consumption.

Preface

I have always enjoyed a good story.

When I was in college I found that, on occasion, words would just come to me. A decade later this became such a problem that, on occasion, I would have to pull over when driving to jot down a story that was manifesting to me at that moment. Another decade later, and at least 250k words of various stories written in various places, I began to exercise my writing by posting shorts online in various places to see if they were enjoyed... or to discover that I was writing garbage.

They were enjoyed. They were far more successful than I expected. This book is a volume that includes some of those stories, compiled with others, to showcase some of my works.

Woken Giant

The General walked into the briefing chamber.

It was obvious from the paleness of the scales that he was very old, old enough that nearly all of the base pigment of his skin had faded into the stark whiteness of old age. Despite his age, his feather tufts were just as healthy as those of a young male, displaying a marvelous plumage indicating virility and fertility.

The dark brown hair protecting his air gills stood in stark contrast against the white scales of his body. The set of slick, brown mats of fur would serve him well to insulate against air: too hot, or too cold, or too dry. This General, it seems, would still be able to take his full 310 cm height into the harshest situations despite his advanced age.

He strode through the assembled crowd to take possession of the presenter's mound in the center of the room. All six of his forward eyes seemed very determined, while the remainder scanned the room in all directions. He had barely set foot atop the presenter's mound when colors started to splash around his countenance, betraying his sense of urgency.

It took but a moment for the central patch between the four upper eyes of everyone in attendance to slip into the telltale orange tone that indicated their attention was his alone.

He began the monologue of color displays instructing everyone in the room of the new danger they had encountered, a new species that had become a major impediment to their colonization efforts.

You are all aware of our customary approach to a new world.

We examine it and determine if there are any indigenous lifeforms that will likely be a nuisance, or even a serious threat, to our efforts. You are also all aware that we leave planets alone that have sentient life; we leave them alone and move along.

We made a mistake.

We found a world upon which there were beings, tiny beings, who had a thriving civilization, but we didn't recognize what they were and what their civilization was. We looked at them the same way we view murtmoffits on this world. They build extensive

colonies out of the local materials, but they are hardly sentient.

We did what we normally do; we began to exterminate them rather than let them become a nuisance to our colony.

They fought back. They fought back hard. They deployed equipment and weaponry that, in many ways, rivals our own. We retreated and left them to their tiny little world.

The most unfortunate aspect of our mistake is that we made it across many worlds at nearly the same time. Many ships, many potential colonies, and many lives were engaged in combat before we realized our mistake. We slaughtered millions of them and lost thousands of our own before we came to realize we should leave them alone.

Having never made such a mistake before, we opted to leave them alone.

Recently, they found us.

Their ships are slow, but incredibly powerful. They have incredible range, and, most importantly, they seem to NEVER run out of fuel.

This species is pursuing a vendetta against us for our mistake, and they keep coming.

Through our many engagements, we have learned very little about them, but it is enough.

We know that they, like us, appear to differentiate through coloring. They *seem to have the very young and the very old working side-by-side. We also know that they vary greatly in size, and that in full colonies, they appear to reach a maximum height of roughly 214 centimeters, but they seem to have no small-size threshold. In the debris of destroyed colonies, we have found specimens as small as 15 centimeters in height. We cannot figure out what these smallest specimens contribute to the colony, but they appear to have a function because they are important enough that the larger specimens often carry them around and protect them during our attacks.*

We have yet to find a reproductive nest. We cannot find any evidence of eggs or larvae of any sort. It

appears that their colonization efforts have yet to establish colonies with nurseries.

We have determined that they communicate with each other, but their skin shades do not change in any pattern we can recognize; we also have found that they cover the majority of their bodies for some reason that we cannot discern.

They also only have two eyes, both in the front of their head. We cannot discern how they function without being able to see in all directions at once. They also have two openings, surrounded by some sort of hard skin flap, on either side of their head. We cannot determine the nature nor function of these apparent organs.

We have established colonies on planets where the entire habitable zone was devoid of these beings only to have them attack us from the frozen polar regions or out of regions that are far too warm to support life. From this we have concluded that they must be able to handle temperatures ranging from -40 through to 50. Their tolerance for these extreme temperatures makes it very difficult for us to take any fighting to them when they have established a foothold in areas that are so hostile. Additionally, we *have found that they appear to have mining colonies on worlds where the highest temperatures barely reach the cold end of their tolerance and, on the other side, colonies on worlds where the temperatures start at their highest temperature tolerance and get warmer.*

We have been caught off guard several times by invasions from neighboring planets in systems that we thought were completely empty.

We have also discovered that mortal wounds do not necessarily remove members of their species from fighting. We have multiple examples of mortal wounds driving a specific individual to extreme levels of aggression in an effort to provide an overall tactical advantage for their team. Unlike us, a mortal wound cannot be considered effective unless the target is fully dead.

We have also witnessed multiple individuals who appear to have had limbs replaced with machinery after suffering a severe injury. We cannot determine how they can integrate the technology into their bodies without the catastrophic impact that such efforts have had in our experiments for limb replacements.

The most important factor that we have observed among the dying members of their species is that they are all insane.

Their emotions appear to outpace their reason in nearly all examples. Individuals will clearly sacrifice themselves to provide a momentary tactical advantage to their comrades. In other instances, teams will refuse to leave any member behind, risking the lives of their soldiers to recover the body of one of their fallen. They will shield the least important of their species, the tiniest ones, and risk the more able-bodied in doing so. They keep coming at us and expending resources to charge farther and farther into our territories even though we have stopped aggressively encroaching on their worlds, only trying to purge contested worlds of their presence.

This conflict is a terrible problem for us, and you should all fear this new enemy because they are coming. Nothing we do and no actions we take seem to have any impact on them. We cannot communicate with them because they don't respond to any message of peace or negotiation that is sent to them. We cannot even determine how they communicate, let alone decipher their communication. We fear that our mistake may have placed us on an irrevocable path toward destruction.

Be prepared. Anything new you can learn about these tiny and insane beings may be the fragment of information we need to surrender to them before they exterminate us.

The Venue

The marquis read "**ONE NIGHT ONLY**" in fixed lettering, but there was no need to put that on the variable signage and waste space. Everything here was a single performance. No artist ever came back to this venue; that was part of how the venue was so successful.

If your favorite artist was here, you had to see them for *THAT* show because you would get no other chance, ever.
Every show was a sold-out show at the venue, too. Each and every ticket went for a premium, and people came from around the world to see the shows that

were put on there.

It was a spectacle. Each and every show was fantastic and pleased everyone in the crowd. There were no negative reviews.

I walked by the venue every day on my way to, and again on my way from, work. I saw who was coming as soon as the sign was updated. I marveled at the names on the sign on a regular basis.

I wished I had had the money to purchase a ticket for the three-night extravaganza with Mozart, Pachelbel, and Bach all being featured prominently, but I simply could not afford it, so I listened from outside the building.

I have had occasion to want the concert in progress to stop as well. When that happens, I take solace in knowing that the artists will be gone the next day and their music with them.

Occasionally they do lectures, too. Those are not as popular although they still always sell out. The presentation of the Gettysburg Address was a marvelous educational opportunity, and it was followed by a discussion on the topic of slavery and the economics of national division and secession. I remember seeing that lecture clearly when I was in school. It was the best field trip we ever had.

This morning, though, was a completely new endeavor posted to their sign. Something daring that will be a spectacle worth seeing. Something unique.

The sign read:
> *TONIGHT ONLY*
> *DUELING ELVIS*

Old Elvis Presley and Young Elvis Presley
Take the Stage Together

This will be amazing.

My one question is whether the knowledge of what Elvis becomes when he gets old will alter how young Elvis lives his life when they are returned to their own time.

I'm guessing that they have that figured out.

The Looking Glass

It was under a sheet in the back of the barn, hidden away.

I asked the owner what it was and why it was hidden.

The response was unnerving and intriguing at the same time, "that's the possessed mirror. You don't want it."

Of course, that made me want it all that much more.

"Can I see it?" I asked, eager to see what could cause such a reaction from a jovial elderly man who was selling antiques out of his disused barn.

"Only if you buy it and take it home. I will not take that sheet off in my presence ever again." A simple but concrete answer.

I bought the mirror without even seeing what it looked like.

I took it home.

I unveiled the mirror in its new home in the back room with all of the other trinkets of no purpose or kept solely for their sentimentality. It was of an interesting design. Its frame was both ornate and simple, carved from what appeared to be granite, yet it did not weigh as though it were granite through and through.

After examining the overall frame, I stepped back to see the full item. In the glass I stood looking back at myself. I looked at myself but something was not quite right, yet I could not place what that something might be. After a few minutes, I decided I must be letting the words of the old man get to me and I went about my business with my chores, errands, and catching up on the TiVo.

Days later I had to go into the back room to look for something. As I walked by the mirror, something caught my eye, so I stopped and turned to look at it again. There I was, just as slightly off as I had been the other day. Then I figured out what it was: the white patch in my beard was on the wrong side. I took a closer look, as did my reflection. We both stood there transfixed by the oddity of the reflection we

were presented until we couldn't resist reaching to touch our white patch... That is when the alarm sounded for each of us. As I reached with my right hand so, too, did my reflection.

We both stopped. We both stood back. All of the movements were exactly the same. Not reflections of each other but as though we were each our own person taking the exact same actions. Instead of seeing a reflection of ourselves, we were seeing a video. The image was NOT reversed as it should be.

We both stopped and stared, jaws hanging open.

Then I noticed something important in the background. All of the writing on everything was also not reversed.

This was not a mirror.

This was ... something else.

A few days later I came back to the looking glass again. I found myself entering at the same time. We both stopped and examined each other thoroughly. We

then stepped "out of frame" and came back with a message on a piece of paper.

The messages both read, "This is not a mirror." Both were displayed correctly.

I stepped out of frame again and came back with a new message; my duplicate also had a paper in his hands. When we flipped them around, both read, "Do something unpredictable."

And we both did jumping jacks and made moose antlers with our hands.

We, obviously, were so close to being each other that our thoughts were the same. We obviously needed something that wasn't tied to our behaviors to experiment with.

I brought my best friend to look into the mirror with me, so did my companion. We found ourselves looking at two sets of people. Two mes and two of her. Staring at each other. We followed the same routine as before with the messages and our friends were as alarmed as we were ... then the mirror shifted.

It was so subtle that I almost did not notice it.

The mirror shifted such that my companion's belt changed color. Nothing else. Just the shift from black to brown of the belt.

I wrote a new note.

"Did you see that?"

The response was "See what?"

Finally: something that was different!

"Your belt color changed for me. You were wearing a black belt like mine to the brown one."

"I've been wearing the brown one all along," was the reply.

"I swear; it changed. Did my belt change to you?" I asked.

"I don't know. I didn't notice it changing. But it is odd that they aren't a match this time."

We proceeded to spend the next fifteen minutes discussing the first mismatch of our experiences and then we all went about our ways.

Days later I caught the looking glass again when I was looking for something. This time it was empty. My partner obviously was not needing the same thing I needed at the same time.

The next time I encountered my partner in the glass, we were wearing different shirts. This seemed to shock and surprise my partner as he held up a message reading "Our shirts are different!"

My reply surprised him as he had no recollection of the belt exchange.

We both arrived at the same conclusion simultaneously and wrote it out: "You're not the same other me."

We then realized that the looking glass was sliding between reflections. It was not showing the same reflection each time, nor were the variants of ourselves being reflected the same.

As we stood there realizing this, he changed. Not much, but enough. His haircut was different, and his beard was trimmed better.

The note response was immediate from both of us "You just changed."

This was alarming ... and fascinating.

All of the mes became transfixed by watching the glass.

When I was not sleeping or at work, I was watching the glass. I was cycling through every variant of me that it would show me.

I came to realize that it was shifting about every 5 minutes. So many mes out there. So many versions. So many changes, and yet we were all pretty much the same.

Then, suddenly, they weren't.

Suddenly there was a me looking at me who was angry. A me whose life had laden him with a bitterness that had created a permanent impression on his face.

A weight on his soul that I could SEE just by looking at him.

He held up a sign that read "I hate you. Why did you get a better life than me?"

I stood there, stunned. I thought about all of the things that could have been worse because of circumstances beyond my control. Situations where I was lucky when it mattered. Situations where the outcome could have changed my life dramatically for the worse if the tiniest of things had gone badly.

I quickly scribbled a sign "I'm sorry things went badly for you. What things were they?"

In response he held up what should have been his right hand. Instead, there was a healed-over mangled stump.

I held up a sign "How?"

His response alarmed me, "Infection from dog attack."

Then the screen shifted again.

This me was equally angry.

So was the next, and the next, and the next.

From this point out they started to get worse and worse.

It was as if the Looking Glass knew. It knew the quality of life, and it calibrated YOU by showing you similar realities before showing you what COULD have happened to you.

I now realize why the old man hated this looking glass.

Seeing all of the misfortune that could have happened to me manifested in reality was traumatic.

My happiness was stolen by the looking glass under the weight of guilt that I had somehow managed to avoid all of the terrible fates that other versions of me had not.

What is it called when you have Survivor's Guilt for your alternate selves?

The worst part is that I can't even begin to tell many people as no one will believe me, and those that might would want to see for themselves.

I don't want them to feel what I feel now.

I don't want them to mourn what happened to alternate versions of themselves.

What I want is for me to be able to see those versions of myself and turn that into celebrating what went right instead.

How do I do that?

How do I forget mangled arms and scarred faces?

How to I forget broken souls?

How do I forget me in a wheelchair?

How do I forget all of the things that might have happened to me that DID to another version of me?

How do I not waste my fortunes lamenting their bad fates?

Humanity Flies

Home is used up
All hopes lie in a new world
To cradle new life

A world has been found
A ship built to get us there
The launch was flawless

Billions of miles out
Home is lost in the darkness
Decades of flight left

The hope of mankind
Slumbers quietly onboard
The future lies ahead

Relaxing in space
Cold sleep systems working
Ship's systems humming

Plink plink thud BAM pfffffffff
The sounds herald disaster
It should be quiet

Multiple impacts
The tiniest particles
Rip through the ship's hull

Loud klaxons sounding
Wake us from our deep slumber
Ship is breaking up

Evacuation
Life pods floating in deep space
Ship disintegrates

Forever falling
The inky blackness surrounds
Alone I will die

Witness

Home is a long way away, longer than anyone who has never been here can imagine.

Scientists and engineers can quote you the distance, and so can a great number of other people, but they don't KNOW how far away it is.

I'm standing here. I KNOW it. They can't imagine the solitude of the moon.

It's quiet here. I like it, and so do all of the others in the base. That's why we were picked, because we like the quiet. Our psych profiles outlined we would likely not go crazy in the moon base for an extended time. We can handle it here.

We can, and we do.

Life here is simple: we rotate through the work that needs to get done, sometimes solo, sometimes in pairs, rarely in a larger group.

Service checks on the antenna and solar array are the two most dangerous and the most solitary jobs we have. I love them because I can put on some tunes and trot across the surface. I can drive the rover. I can simply enjoy my thoughts and the view of the universe.

We only get to go outside about once a month because that's the rotation. One crew member does the rounds each week. The rest of the chores are all done inside. Even servicing the harvesters is done in the garage for safety reasons. It's simply easier to work with the tools in a pressurized environment. Faster, safer, easier. So that's what we do.

So, I enjoy my monthly trip outside. I take my time. We're allowed to spend the whole day doing it, and I always do; Jim holds the record for completing it the fastest because, unlike me, he HATES it out here.

I drive the rover around and take in the sights. The never-changing sights. I look at the stars. I watch the positions of the other planets in the sky. And, most importantly, I watch home. Home is a brilliant sight as it hangs in the air. I remember seeing the photos taken from the moon by the first men here, but they don't compare to the reality. I've even replicated their shots, and still, I cannot come close to the same level of awe that I feel just standing there myself.

Every month I celebrate the beauty and glory of the world below me. I celebrate it with equal parts longing and dread. The longing because it is home and it is so far away; the dread because to return to home means I have to leave here. I would have to surrender my solitude and quiet for the noise of the world.

Usually, our rounds are uneventful. We do inspections on everything and ensure the dust hasn't worked its way into anything important. We check for micrometeorite impacts that our seismic detectors didn't catch.

This time, though, one of the panels had a fresh punch all the way through it. I look around and I see a few other mini craters littering the surface. A small gravel field must have been floating in space and we caught up with it.

I radio in the panel damage and I begin to dismount it for repairs in the garage.

That's when the thud shutters through my feet.

I look up to see a plume of dust floating around the surface in a cloud.

Another thud.

I know what is happening. More space debris.

We have shelters on the surface for this. Concrete bunkers that are, basically, just large enough to stand in in the event of a micrometeorite shower. I curse and I stand in it.

"Control, the shower doesn't appear to be over. I'm in the shelter" I report calmly as I stare through the inky abyss toward Earth.

Watching carefully, I can see glints of sunlight reflecting off the larger stones as they pass through the space above me. I know that the largest of these would be a serious problem to us if they hit in the wrong place, and I am pleased they sail on by. It occurs to me, while watching this, that I should document it. I setup the camera and start filming.

Tiny rocks and slightly less tiny rocks streak by between the backdrop of Earth and the camera lens.

That's when I see it.

A large rock.

I can't tell how far away it is. It could be of moderate size and really close or enormous and really far away. I can't help but stare as it tumbles across the sky.

I point the camera toward it to record its passing when I realize, with utter horror, what I am seeing.

The edges of the rock start to glow slightly and gas jets start to plume off the rock in a variety of directions. The coloring grows and the rock's size is suddenly apparent.

This rock is enormous, and it is glowing with atmospheric friction from

Earth.

This rock is on a collision course.

It is a matter of milliseconds from when I realize this until the impact itself, but those ticks of time pass with increasing slowness due to the shock of comprehension.

Home was about to die.

The impact ripped a hole in my reality.

The plume rippled outward, and the heat and shock-wave traversed the globe.

I watched the colors change.

I watched entire cloud fronts get pushed away.

I watched the vast hurricane that was roaming the equatorial region be obliterated by the force of the new energy.

The destruction cascaded across the globe, leaving a fiery wake across the land and a steamy fog where there were supposed to be tranquil seas.

"Uh, guys?" I quietly spoke into my radio.

"Yes, Heather?" was the reply. Jim's voice registered confusion over my lack of protocol in my message.

"We have a problem."

"We know, the solar panel."

"No. We have a bigger problem. Home is gone."

"What do you mean?"

"I mean Earth is gone. We're alone. I just watched the end of life on Earth."

The Reality Bomb

The lab is a haphazard setup in the basement of the giant home.

Years of scrounging the cast offs of the more sophisticated labs and manufacturing firms have allowed this home to host an amazing lab for an independent scientist. Pretty much any machine that is needed is available albeit some are several generations out of date.

Behind the lab is a storage room filled with shelving. The shelves are filled with a variety of prototypes of inventions dating back nearly a century. Most of them never worked, but the few that did generated the income to continuously improve the laboratory over time.

The contents of the storage room, the lab, and the home that contained them, both belong, now, to the "best invention ever," of the man who built it: his daughter.

Now appearing to be in her 60s, her wild, unkempt hair is a white mane that is barely controlled by whatever restraint she applies to it while working.

Her career, thus far, has exceeded the scope of her father's. His early assistance and always having the lab available have allowed her to invent more things faster than her father ever could. She has had many successes, allowing her revenue stream to expand at a pace that allows her continued efforts.

But she has had many failures, too. Unlike her father, she takes her failed inventions into the world rather than racking them in the storage room. When he used to unveil a product, the community stood in awe, waiting with eagerness, for whatever it was he was to present. When she presents a product, the community laughs at her. They wait for the failure and are shocked when a product is successful.

Her father always tried to teach her that "showmanship" was as important as the science itself, but it was a lesson she had continuously failed to learn.

"I'll show them, I'll show them all" is the mantra that is heard in the lab when she is working. "Laugh at me, will they? Well, I'll give them something to laugh at!"

The Press Conference was packed. Dozens of reporters, accompanied by their photographers and a healthy number of videographers, filled the room to watch the newest complete failure of "that crazy old lady scientist." They were all prepared to watch the failure and boost their ratings by sharing the results of the failure with their audiences. This lady, if nothing else, was always a fantastic source for comedic segments to air between the harshest of realities that the world needed to have broadcast to them.

Standing about three feet tall, at the head of the room, stood a shiny metal podium of sorts. An overhead camera captured the downward view onto the invention and projected it on the giant screen behind it, giving the impression to all in-attendance that the podium was a metallic C with the opening facing away from them. At the center of the C lay a single red circle, which to everyone present appeared to be a big button.

There was no other evidence of controls. No posters. No handouts. Nothing. Just the large metallic C podium with its big red button.

The time ticked away slowly, everyone's eagerness for the presentation to begin causing a relativistic cascade of the perception of time. Seconds lengthened into eternities as the clock ticked inexorably onward and everyone in attendance exhausted their speculative commentary on what this ridiculous contraption could be.

Precisely one minute late for the start of the conference, the "crazy scientist" entered the back door and silently walked to her place within the podium. She smiled. Her smile carried a beacon of insanity in it, a measure of craziness that broadcast itself into the entire audience, generating a universal intake of breath from all in attendance. "Good afternoon, everyone. I'm glad you all came to see my newest invention. I know some of you," she glared at a few specific reporters in the room, "came for the 'great pleasure' of watching another of my inventions fail miserably. I know some of you came," again, her penetrating gaze wandered around the room, locking eyes with select members of the media, "because you expected to be able to report on how stupid the idea is and why it was a complete and ridiculous waste of my time to even pursue it in the first place. But, today, I want to assure you all that the major result of this invention will affect you all tremendously. You won't be laughing at this one. I guarantee it."

A slight chorus of laugher and chuckles echoed around the room, as a variety of those in attendance failed to suppress their mirth at her claims.

"This button, once pressed, will vindicate everything I have ever strived for. In a single motion, I will silence all of your derisions against my life's work, and I will stand triumphant in my mastery of the scientific principles of the universe."

No one tried to contain their laughter at this incredible boast. The laughter rose through the crowd as ripples spread out from the surface of a pond. The scientist's smile grew with the laughter. "I'm glad you are so amused by my comments. It makes what is about to happen so much sweeter."

She pressed the red button, and at first, no one in the audience thought anything happened. The laughter started to increase in volume, but a wave of silence spread out from the podium. An unnatural silence as the very constructs of sound unraveled around the people in the front row. The laughter from everyone else turned to gasps as the very threads of reality unraveled before their eyes.

The projection screen and wall behind the podium dissolved into a black void of nothingness as the first row of the audience silently screamed their final moments of existence. The wave continued outward, enveloping the entire press conference and then the entire building. The wave continued, unmaking all that existed in every direction, leaving the psychotic scientist floating in her podium at the center of a realm of growing nothingness that ate away all of the world, then the very space itself that the world had occupied.

The nothingness grew until it didn't, allowing reality to crash back into the hole that the scientist had ripped through the fabric of space-time. The very fabric of space-time snapping closed around her left her a mere moment to understand her mistake as the air was ripped from her into the vast vacuum of emptiness that hung where the earth used to be.

One second.

Two seconds.

Three seconds.

Thirty seconds.

A full minute.

The scientist's pain grew as her blood boiled inside her. Her lungs ruptured as the air forced itself to ever-growing dimensions in the lack of pressure. Her skin expanded and bloated as the vacuum gave license to all of her interior parts to expand at their leisure.

Wordlessly, she tried to mutter her final thought as her eyes glazed over from the damage of the vacuum of space. "Another failure," her lips moved to make the words, but the words themselves failed to come forth.

The scientist floated, the only evidence that humanity had ever existed, inside her metallic podium. The Reality Bomb having detonated its wave of unmaking in a manner that exceeded all of the scientist's expectations.

The Park

There were two groups of children in the neighborhood. There were a lot of other children, too, but there were two GROUPS of children. The groups had been around so long that none of them really knew how the situation got started, and none of them cared.

Each of these groups laid claim to the playground that straddled the border between their respective sections of the neighborhood. Each felt that the other group shouldn't be there.

Neither had a problem with the unaligned children using the playground.

Peace, tranquility, and children's laughter would reign over the playground so long as representation within it included less than a member from each group.

When both groups were present, it all changed.

There was pushing. There was name-calling. There was forced "keep away" with belongings.

There was touch football that rivaled any high school varsity game but without the padding.

Bloody noses. Ripped clothing. Broken toys.

The behavior was out of control.

Both sides claimed they left the other children alone, but there were many incidents of hurt boys and girls who got in the way.

Adults tried to intervene multiple times, but the truces never held beyond the vacancy created when all adults left.

Sometimes it was merely a single insult that ignited the fighting again, other times a physical assault.

This went on for years. Children aged out of the groups and tired of the weariness that the constant battle for the playground brought. New children replaced them. Some children stopped going to the playground because they could while others had nowhere else to go.

Over the years the situation escalated. Bloody noses turned into broken arms; torn clothes turned into

missing articles that the victim had to return home without. Broken toys went from an occasional accident to intentional acts.

The adults merely stood by and chastised the behavior.

The children learned about "tagging" and started marking, then re-marking, then re-marking again the various equipment on the playground.

The park went to ruin as the maintenance could not be completed on pace with the vandalism.

Eventually, the taxpayers who supported the park had had enough.

An ultimatum was issued to all of the children in the neighborhood.

A cease-fire was declared by the adults. The plea was simple: stop this nonsense or we will stop it for you.

That the children would all pay dearly if the adults had to stop it was left unsaid; all of the children knew that reality from their own homes.

At first, it appeared that the cease-fire would hold.

Children played in the park without incident. One group stayed on one side and the other on the opposing side. The unaligned children moved about as they wished.

The cease-fire lasted an eternity.

A whole week passed without incident.

Then a boy from one group wanted to use the swings on the side where the other group was. He got on them and up to swinging speed when the insults started.

Calls of "Jump off, sissy!" and "You won't jump; you're too scared." kicked it off, but the boy swung on.

The group could tolerate the presence of the opposing side but not being ignored.

Within moments the boy was surrounded and someone grabbed his foot.

He slipped from the swing and fell to the ground.

The wind was knocked out of him, and he couldn't breathe. He wanted to cry but could not.

The group laughed and laughed at his sad frame as it lay in the swing's path, the swing flying back and forth over his body.

When he could get up, he found he had a bloody nose and his ankle hurt badly. He cried as he limped home.

The adults gathered the children and told them that they had failed their last chance to keep their playground.

The following Saturday the construction equipment dug up every last piece of play equipment, and a tall fence was installed around the entire area.

The feuding had cost them all that which they loved and had been feuding about.

The message came from the heavens. A simple message. A message directed at the leaders of the world.

The message was unequivocally clear and delivered in all of the languages of the Earth.

"Stop your destructive nonsense or we will stop it for you."

The adults of the world failed to understand the implications of the message.

Momentary Reflection

CLICK.

Nothing happened.

He was still aware, and he thought it should be over already.

Still, nothing happened.

He tried to look around and found that he could not.
He could not move.

Still, nothing happened.

He tried to open his eyes and succeeded.

The lids opened painfully slow, revealing the horror that he had just imparted upon the room.

He could do nothing but look straight ahead with his eyes, staring right at them.

He tried to close his eyes but they would not respond.

Still, nothing happened.

The two corpses lay on the bed in front of him.

The barrel of the gun, a wisp of smoke still frozen in a curl out of the end of it, pointed its maw up at his face.

That maw should have expelled the release from the pain of his life already; he shouldn't be able to contemplate why he is able to contemplate his continued existence.

His wife and child lay, lifeless, in front of him, dead by his own hand.

The reality of what he had done caught up with him, and the emotions were overwhelming.

His wife. His child. He had murdered them in a fit of rage.

The remorse swelled through him, and he broke inside, but he could not weep.

He could not blink. He could not move.

He was frozen in time, staring at the hideous crime he had committed.

There was a flash, and he diverted his attention.

The primer in the shell that would end him was firing.

Its instantaneous reaction was dragging out intolerably.

He watched the flash as it moved past him.

He watched that flash for hours, perhaps days.

It had been a distraction from the soul-rending pain of staring at those whom he had mercilessly slaughtered.

Hours or days passed with no change.

His memory raced, he was forced to see all of the good times he had had with his wife and child, each memory slaughtered by the image of them dead on the bed, covered in gore and blood.

Memories shredded and slaughtered just as he had done to their lives and bodies in reality.

The memories were eaten by the present, and his soul wept inside.

His rage turned on himself.

His hatred of the world burned itself out and turned into a self-loathing that would drive any man to die.

He wanted to kill himself and realized he already had. He was just waiting for it to finish.

The first indicator of the recoil began pushing on his hand.

Years passed to him, still staring at the horror he had imparted on his family.

All the while the results of the trigger pull were slowly working their way down the barrel of the gun.

Decades passed, perhaps even a century.

The concussive wave of sound hit his face.

He still did nothing but stare, in silence, at what he had done.

He suffered more in the milliseconds between the trigger pull and the lead shot hitting his face than he had in all his life.

The shot ripped into his face at the same pace it had traveled from the shell casing to it.

The pace allowed for him to feel each and every rip and tear of his flesh as the shot passed through.

100 separate projectiles with 100 individual paths ripped through his face, inciting pain as they went.

Another century passed as the pain continued.

The leading pellets passed into his skull, splintering slivers into his brain as they punched through.

He could not feel the pain in his brain, but he was suddenly aware of numbness in various parts of his body as the shot and debris shredded his sensory sections.

Memories evaporated as parts of his brain were destroyed.

He felt his very being getting ripped to shreds, his soul being destroyed with the passing of the lead.

The world was ripped from him as the visual cortex was destroyed.

He was in silence and darkness, and there he remained for all time.

The last thing he witnessed was his own blood splattering into the frame that contained his dead family.

Time no longer had any meaning for him.

Each picosecond was an eternity that he was forced to reflect on the last image he had seen with what was left of his mind.

Someday, the slow passage of time would allow him to die and release him from the torment that he had inflicted upon himself through his actions.

This, he realized, is why suicides go to Hell. Hell comes to them while they wait to die.

Empty

When I said I felt empty inside, everyone expressed to me that it is a normal feeling, that everyone feels that way at times. At first, I accepted this and pondered how everyone could feel so isolated and alone all the time, so empty, so insignificant and still maintain a society in which we all lived.

I watched, and I learned, and I came to realize that what I felt was different. It was stronger and more real than that which anyone else felt. Some, perhaps, felt something deep inside them that was gnawing at their psyche the way I feel my soul gnaws on the insides of my body. The depth of the loneliness and emptiness cannot be measured; it cannot be quantified; it cannot be explained.

No one seems to understand that I feel it worse than anyone else, and when I say that, they tell me that that is how everyone feels and that it is normal.

After years of managing the emptiness, I still feel the same; and everyone still tells me that it is normal.

I began, some time ago, to try and walk away the emptiness at night, in the dark, alone.

When the mugger's blade pierced my side, it became apparent how empty I really was. The piercing blow broke the bubble of my skin that contained an event horizon, and the blade, the hand, and the entire mugger were crushed through the resulting hole in my side as the singularity deep inside me consumed him.

I'm sure his death was an eternity of pain and suffering and time slowed down for him as his body was ripped apart, atom by atom, into the never-ending cavity of my soul.

Fortunately for all, I heal fast; only the mugger and some random street rubbish were hauled into the abyss of my entrails this time.

I can't possibly believe that everyone feels this pressure inside them; if they did, there would be stories in the news of people's souls eating the world around them when they were wounded.

I MUST be something different.

But what am I?

Knowing I am different makes me feel that much more alone which, in turn, makes me feel that much more empty inside.

Immortality

There's one thing I don't know. One valuable piece of information that I need:

How to die.

I know how to kill, and thus, I know how dying works, but it doesn't work for me.

Believe me, I've tried.

I've been around a long time, so long I can't remember being a kid. I can't remember growing up. I can't distinguish my earliest memories. They were all a giant jumbled mess long before cybernetics allowed for the archival of memories to make them permanently available.

I could have been a thousand by the time that came about or ten thousand or anywhere in between, perhaps even older.

History is really fuzzy on how long mankind has been around and my memories are so faded that I'm fuzzier on the topic than the best speculations.

But none of that really matters.

I'm old. Very old.

And I'm tired.

It was about a thousand years ago that I wanted to die; I was ready to be done.

So, I tried.

Guns didn't work. Knives. Plasma. Vacuum. Gravity.
Nothing.

Some things were far more painful than others, but I always reconstituted and healed.

And I felt EVERY moment of the pain.

The more drastic the actions, the greater the pain. None of it worked.

I'm going to try something more drastic than anything I've experienced yet. Hopefully, it will free me from the burden of existence.

If you're listening to this, know I chose to make this course correction. I did this deliberately.

I have hope that the sun can finish what nothing else has been able to.
I hope it will burn away this ship and this body to leave me free from my life that has been too long as it is.

Appended to this recording will be all of the data my ship could collect and transmit up until the last moments. I hope it brings valuable insight into the scientific community.

Here's, hopefully, to nothing!

Programming Oversight

The debris field was varied in size and shape, clearly indicating that the explosion had rent the hull apart from the inside, scattering shrapnel from the point of origin outward through the remainder of the ship, all while shearing the very ship itself in twain.

"Control, this is Rescue 17. We have found the debris field. We confirm. We have found the debris field. Field is traveling in line with the last known velocity of the ship. The incident appears to have been internal, rather than externally originated. Seeking the flight controller."

"Roger that, Rescue 17. All other units, abandon search and return to base."

Sifting through the debris is laborious and monotonous. It is boring. There is nothing exciting about finding another dismembered, frozen finger floating in space after you've done so 11,462 times in your career. It is all rote repetition. But we do it anyway. It's important to sort through debris and clear it out of the space lanes to prevent future accidents. It's important to understand design flaws and system failures that claim the lives of crews so that the

Corporation can prevent problems in the future. It's important to return SOMETHING to the families of the expired crew members for their own closure; at least, it is when we can.

"Captain, it looks like we have tractored in all of the debris. The lane should be clear now. Permission to close the outer doors?"

"Permission granted."

I closed the doors and watched their majestic movement close out the stars behind them, the sounds of their machinery vibrating through my feet and up through my suit. The smaller debris still floated through the hold, easily wandering off on various trajectories influenced by leaking magnetic fields and small collisions with each other, but none of it is dangerous to those of us sorting in the hold because we are moving at the same speed as the junk.

"All right, crew" let's start sorting. Bonus replicator rations for whoever finds the flight recorder!"

The search lasted 15 hours before someone found the recorder. In that time we accounted for all of the crew, only two of whom were intact. One was on the

bridge and the other in their quarters, both killed by decompression rather than being torn apart. Seeing their bloated bodies with frozen boils on their skin where their blood boiled inside as they died makes me believe I would rather die quickly, like those as "ground zero" of an event like this. I took the recorder to the records room, leaving the rest of the crew to sort through the remaining garbage.

"Alright, Harry, let's see what went wrong" I said, as I handed the shiny bluish, silvery cube over to my communications expert.

"Sure thing" he said, dropping it into the slot. The holographic display shined to life, showing a cacophony of interlinked lines, texts, and numbers, all streaming along in a gibberish that I will never be able to understand, but Harry does, and that's what is important.

"You're not going to believe this"

"I need to. We don't have much choice, do we?"

"I guess not, but this is the most ridiculous thing I have ever heard of."

"What's that?"

"Italian night."

"What?"

"The destruction of the ship was caused by Italian night."

"What does that even mean?"

"Ok, look here," Harry said, scrolling the displays fast enough to induce nausea, "There are MANY log entries here about how they're going to sit down, as a crew, and share one big meal together, rather than all getting their own thing. Sort of weird, but whatever."

"OK. So how did that blow up their ship?"

"So," scrolling again "when the day came, it appears that everyone was responsible for using their replicator rations to make one specific dish that they liked."

"You're not explaining how this wrecked their ship, Harry."

"I'm getting to it. It's so ridiculously stupid that I need to lay the groundwork first."

"Get on with it"

"So here," he said, pointing at a point in the squiggles and lines, "is where someone ordered garlic bread, and here," scrolling the display around again, "someone ordered tomato sauce." Again Harry's fingers flung the data around in ways that nature abhorred "And over here we have several different pasta dishes, each with their own spice and herb mixtures, each with different pasta shapes... What's up with that, by the way, why are there so many?"

"I have no idea."

"Anyway, here is some other sauce, called 'alfredo' and here is a giant bowl of salad."

"And how does this explain the incident?"

"I'm getting there. This is where someone ordered a beverage, and here, here is the very last entry in everything before the ship went kaboom."

"Ok, what is it?"

"Antipasta."

"What?"

"Antipasta. Which, by looking at these logs," he said, pointing to some red lines in a corner of the display, "the computer interpreted WAY wrong. Instead of making some sort of pasta dish as intended, it, literally, crafted the pasta out of anti-atoms. It, literally, made antimatter pasta rather than antepasta. As soon as it materialized, the air touched it and ka-BOOM! The mess hall was gone, tearing the ship apart and keeping us employed."

"You're saying the replicator accidentally misinterpreted a command and blew up the ship by accidentally making antimatter?"

"Yep. That's what I'm saying."

"File the report. I'm going to go make sure no one orders any antepasta on this ship."

Regression

Dearest Anna,

I know this tale is far-fetched and that you won't believe it for a moment, but I must explain my reasons for leaving nonetheless. I'm sorry that I must abandon you in this way, but I, truly, do not belong here, and I must try to find my way back to where I do belong. The weight of the changes has grown too great for me to bear and ignore, and I MUST have answers or face the infinite void of death in my effort to understand.

My tale of woe has been ongoing for some time, so long that I am not sure whence it actually began. At first, I thought it was a problem with my mind, but eventually, things happened often enough that I knew it was not, in fact, me, but rather the world itself that was changing.

I died yesterday.

I woke up this morning, again, with you as though nothing had happened, but it did. I died yesterday, and it was not the first time I have died. I am CERTAIN I have died 57 times now, but it could be several

more, and that is not the part I think you will have the most difficulty believing.

You see, the world shifts every time I die. Something is always a bit more backward and primitive. Each and every time I lose something I took for granted and have to learn how to work within a world without that specific convenience. The first time I am aware I died, and I know now that I died, I was randomly struck by lightning on a clear day. I woke at home next to you the following morning as though nothing had happened. No one knew anything about it. No one thought the previous day had been strange. No one had tended to me. There was no evidence I had died. The only thing that seemed amiss to me was that everyone kept asking me about my phone. You see, according to all of them, my phone was the newest model on the market and the most amazing piece of technology yet released. But, to me, it was the very same phone I had been working with for 5 years, albeit brand new. The date was right, but people were acting as though the entire world of technology was 5 years behind where I knew it to be. It is at this point in my writing, dearest Anna, that I know you must be terribly confused about what I mean by a phone in this context. You see, where I come from is a much more advanced world than the

one in which we have been residing. I know you have read about telephones in the newspaper and how they are "all the rage" in the cities these days but have never seen one yourself. Where I come from, they are, truly, "all the rage," so much so that nearly everyone has one in their pocket at all times. The phones do not require wires, and they do MUCH more than just allow someone to talk from great distances. In fact, believe it or not, most people abhor using the phone in that manner and prefer to use the phone to write short letters back and forth instead! The difference being that those letters are delivered instantly, anywhere in the world! Marvelous and unbelievable, I know ... but it is the reality where I came from. I lived in that world for about five years before I died.

Each time I wake from having died, the date is the same. The years have fled from my body, and I am, once *again, the age I was when I first died. The date is always the same, and I live my life from that day onward in the new world as though I had always been there; the world does not know any different ... but I always do.*

I died yesterday, after spending 17 years with you in a world where we had a telephone in our home. You thought it was silly when I woke one morning and

decided we should get one. You thought it was frivolous for us to spend the money to have one of those devices in our home when no one else in town had one yet. But, very quickly, the technology spread among the people we live with. They found it invaluable to be able to call the store and see if they had the item they needed or to call a friend and see if they were home before going to visit them. For years, before I died yesterday, the marvels of the modern world as you knew them fascinated all of the people we know. But then I died and that world was erased like those before it.

I have written this letter to you several times through the course of my journey, each time as painful to me as the others and, each time, in a different medium. Each time it is written with the tools available to me, this time with this simple quill and on this paper. The last time I wrote this letter I typed it neatly on a typewriter, for they were plentiful and easy to come by. The first time I wrote this letter I wrote it on a device similar to a typewriter in many ways, but much more advanced: a device called a "computer" (no, not like Frank, who does math for the government, but a device that replaced Frank's entire profession). That was the last world in which computers existed, for when I was run

over by a car three weeks into my journey, I woke to find a world where computers had yet to be invented.

I am so sorry that I must leave you but I must travel the world to see if there are any others who remember the world differently from how it is. I must find answers to what is happening to me, and I must see if there is some purpose to why I am deposited into a strange reality each time I die. I must know if there is someone out there killing me to make it happen.

I am sorry I must leave you, it is the epitome of unfairness that you should pay the price for my misfortune but know that I love you and I take solace in knowing that, when I next die, I will awaken next to you in yet another world where everything has rewound just a bit more.

Lastly, electric lights are very much worth it. When you have the opportunity, I suggest you have them installed. You won't believe how much they change the world.

The Replacement Engineers

I overheard the others discussing what species were best for what jobs and I heard them laughing at the idea of humans being worth anything, so I had to intrude upon their jovial intercourse. "Excuse me, but I couldn't help overhearing your chat about what species are best in what positions on a ship. Mind if I join you to tell you a tale?"

As I was only familiar with one of the languages being used at the table, it took a moment for my universal translator to update and present their assent to me.

"Excellent. Let me tell you the tale of when I met my first humans."

I found myself needing an engineer because mine had rolled into his dormancy cycle while on shift, three months ahead of expectations, so I had to stop at a spaceport and ship it back to Krag'neckor. While there I had to find a new engineer to continue because, as we all know, flying without one is a way to summon all of the technical problems of the universe onto your ship.

So, there I was, looking through the available talent on the station, becoming increasingly discouraged at the lack of quality ... anything, when I stumbled on a pair-bonded set of humans, Michael and Karina, looking to join a crew headed anywhere so long as they could get off the station. I called the com listed and set up a meeting with them.

I was surprised when they arrived. I had always heard humans were small, but I was not really prepared for how much smaller than normal they are. Together they barely made the minimum mass for entry into our spacing guild, but there were two of them and I was desperate, so I decided to give them a chance because they, between them, had the minimum engineering certifications I needed. I asked them what special environmental conditions they needed, and they assured me that anything on my ship should be "Something they can work with."

They easily fit into the vacated quarters for the ship's engineer, and they were happy to share the quarters. They hauled all of their own belongings onto the ship. When given the introduction to the

remainder of the crew, they were very personable and friendly. They even promised to "kill boredom" with us by teaching us some "games." All in all, it sounded

very odd and different, but none of us

cared so long as they could keep us in the sky when needed.

The weird part began when we toured the ship. As we all know, the optimal temperature for water and carbon life forms is approximately 20 degrees. That is, of course, the temperature that I keep my ship at, and while some of my crew prefer 1 or two degrees in either direction, it is a universally accepted temperature for everyone in the public areas of the ship. The humans were no different in this regard. The weird part, though, is when we got to engineering. I showed them the environmental suit storage bin as I got mine out of storage and began putting it on. That's when Karina asked if there was a radiation leakage problem. I, of course, was horrified. I would never allow such a thing to go unmitigated on MY ship, and I told her so. She then asked why I was putting on an envirosuit to go into engineering.

I was dumbfounded. How could beings with certifications in engineering not know why I needed an environmental suit to enter such a hot environment? It

was nearly 48 degrees in there! I wouldn't last long enough to give them a tour of engineering, let alone work in there, without an envirosuit to keep me cool.

So, I replied that it's to protect me from the extreme heat of the engine room. Michael then asked what level of heat I am speaking of, and when I told him, they looked at each other and shrugged ... and then went in. No envirosuit. They just walked into the engine room unprotected!

I struggled, in the clumsy suit, to follow them into the blast furnace of the engine room as they looked around and identified all of the components needed to keep the ship operating. I, in the suit, began feeling the effects of the extreme heat almost immediately and they, if any change actually happened at all, just looked like they were a bit damp. That's it. They, truly, *did not care about the heat; it was nothing to them.*

Time passed. They were with my ship for about a year and made use of the synthrec room together often. None of us ever bothered them when they were using that space, and none of us ever asked them what they were doing in there. None of our business and we all made use of the synthrec room for a variety of

purposes ourselves. It was a great way to visit a favorite place or do some exercise or even to eat favorite foods that we couldn't experience any other way, even if the calories were false and provided no nutritional value. They taught us many of their "games," and we discovered that they were a pleasant novelty to fill the down-time. I came to particularly like one of their simple games which they called "Reversi." We shared our literature and music with them and they with us. You would be amazed at how varied their music is. There truly is nothing ... quite like it.

But, anyway, I digress. It was about a year that they were with us, doing an admirable job at preventative maintenance and fixing any issues that arose, when Howler pirates attacked us. We tried to run and failed, and my ship was not equipped to fight them in ship-to-ship combat, so I relented and surrendered to them. As they approached for docking, I advised my crew what was happening. Michael approached me and asked if I was really just going to let the Howlers win and take all our cargo. I gently, but firmly, informed Michael that I had no alternative because I could not fight them as the ship was not equipped to do so. I outlined that it was too costly to allow a firefight on my ship and that the loss of cargo was less expensive

than the repairs such an effort would incur. Michael seemed extremely agitated by this. He did not like the idea of "letting them get away with it." I advised him that I did not like the idea either but I had no recourse. That's when he smiled. He said, "What if I take the fight onto THEIR ship?"

Dumbfounded, his question horrifying me to my very core, I replied, "But you can't! It's far too cold on their ship. You'll freeze!"

He looked at me, glared right into my face, and said, "Let me worry about that."

I stared, dumbfounded and replied, "You know that their ship is -30 degrees, right? That Howlers come from a world that is frozen ice, and they have special adaptations that allow them to survive in that world, including heavy layers of blubber and a thick fur pelt. You know this, right? You have neither a layer of blubber nor a thick coat of fur. You, clearly, are used to an environment warmer than standard since you can go in the engine room for hours at a time without protection. You won't survive in there."

Again, he replied, "Let me worry about that. I'm doing it unless you, specifically, order me not to.

Someone has to teach these jackals a lesson, and it might as well be Karina and me."

Again, I was dumbfounded. Not only was he proposing he risk his life but, also, that of his bonded partner. I was speechless. Before I could even think to tell him "no," he turned and left with a "Thanks, Boss. You won't regret this."

The Howlers demanded that all crew join in our Mess Hall, unarmed, so that we wouldn't be able to try anything, and that's where I, and the rest of the crew besides Michael and Karina, went.

The sounds of the Howler ship attaching to Airlock 3 could be heard reverberating throughout the ship and that's when we heard Karina yell, "They're on Airlock 3!" followed a moment later by the two of them running past the entrance to the Mess Hall in some strange attire that I had not seen before. It looked as though they had strapped fuel tanks of some sort to their banks and were carrying strange-looking, tool-like objects in their hands as though they were weaponry. The sound of running changed and Michael reappeared for a moment with a HUGE toothy expression on his face, he pointed the weapon-looking thing in the air and let out two quick bursts of intense

fire toward the ceiling before laughing and running back toward Karina.

I don't know exactly what they did, but the exact moment the airlock door broke its seal, altering the pressure in my vessel slightly, the screams began. I say screams because that is what they were, not the usual Howls that the Howlers make to communicate but high-pitched yips and barks of terror and pain. There was another pressure change, and then a draft of extremely cold air began to flow across the floors of my ship. We closed the door to the Mess Hall to keep the cold out.

And we waited. We waited for the Howlers to come take vengeance upon us for daring to defy them.

Then the door opened again. It was Karina. Her goofy-looking garment was covered in blood and gore. She smiled at us and said "Coast is clear. Captain, you've got yourself a second ship if you want it. We even turned up the thermostat for you."

I, quite cautiously, left the Mess Hall. There were dead Howlers in the airlock, and the door to their ship was closed. The air was cold, too cold, but I knew my life support systems would rectify that quickly enough. I asked Karina "Where's Michael?"

She replied "Oh, he's in there," indicating the other side of the airlock, "getting some food. They have some great menu items that we haven't had a chance to have on this ship. Why let it go to waste?"

So, that is the tale of my time with some humans. You might think they're puny and weak, but they are not. It turned out that both Karina and Michael were only MINIMALLY trained in engineering as a SIDE JOB for their real vocation. They were both trained in the human space force as "special forces" soldiers, and the engineering training was a hobby they both enjoyed as well as a backup in case a human space navy ship they were on lost too many engineers. Yes, that's right, their high-quality engineering work was just their side hobby. Their real vocation was killing, and they, just two humans, dispatched an entire Howler pirate crew of 20 by themselves ... on the Howler ship in the Howler temperatures. They solidified my respect for humans that day, and my fear. I decided to give them the Howler ship when we reached the next port, and I sought a more conventional, stable, and predictable engineer replacement. So, now that I have told *my tale, I urge you to not laugh at humans. They are tiny, yes, but any of them out here in space are of a hardy stock that is absolutely terrifying when they are faced with any sort of adversity.*

Bears

Council, we come begging for your help.

As you all know we are a species who reside at the edges of our oceans. Our race has a lineage that left the seas for land and then, eons later, returned to the seas as our primary homes. We venture forth to the land as needed, but spend the majority of our lives in the water.

We farm deep in our seas. We hunt in our seas. We build in our seas. As a general rule, we only venture 100 kilometers from the coastline, leaving everything farther from the shore a pristine nature preserve.

Before I get to my specific request, I must outline the events that led up to our current state. As you know, the humans are technologically primitive and manage to venture to the stars in ships we would barely dare to use to visit a neighboring planet. The moment they reach a point of a technology's usefulness, they explore every avenue of the technology, push it to its very limits, and often have disastrous accidents, but this does not stop them. They refuse to learn the lesson of caution and just keep misusing ... everything.

There was a particularly volatile member of my race who made some disparaging remarks about humans and their ships while in a recreation facility on a way station. One of the humans did not appreciate the remarks and commented back. I regret to acknowledge that, at some point in the proceedings, the member of my race physically assaulted the human. This, of course, was a serious breach of protocol and, more importantly, a terrible mistake. I have seen the holos of the event. The human, enraged by the assault and standing on the higher moral high ground of defense, fought back. Other members of my race joined the first, and the single human fought them all. Her crew mates stood by and watched, waiting to see if there was any need to intervene, but there was not. The one human female trounced four of my race, beating them so *severely they spent a decaday in their medical facility. As far as I can tell from the holo, the human female was unharmed, but we will never know.*

The state of the four placed in medical care, and taken out of work rotations, outraged the Captain of their vessel such that they fired upon the unarmed human freighter upon which the humans were serving. An armed human transport moved in to protect the freighter, and both ships were destroyed. The remainder of the freighters in that convoy fled.

This incident was regrettable but stemmed from a personal conflict between individuals. Those responsible for the altercation on the station and the personnel who fired upon the human vessels have been punished accordingly through our legal system. We thought that was the end of it. We were wrong.

We were very wrong.

An automated courier beacon appeared in our home system 37 days later. It began to broadcast a simple message on repeat, "You fired on an unarmed freighter vessel without provocation. This is considered an act of war. In the interest of ongoing peace, we are allowing you one cycle to answer for this event via diplomatic means." The beacon was active for one day before it self-destructed.

The homeworld thought the message was a prank and didn't bother to reply. That, it turns out, was our third huge mistake; our first mistake was underestimating the humans in every way; the second was the incident that triggered the message. Our fourth mistake was assuming that we were impervious to any form of attack, that our homeworld defenses would detect and eliminate, any threat long before we had to worry about it.

We have all seen that the humans will fight in a head-on approach with a viciousness unknown by any other race. They are worse than any cornered animal when pushed to combat. We have all seen, and are terrified of, how the humans can turn any technology into an overt weapon AND how they often have means of converting any system on their ships into one should they need to do so. We have all been informed of the violent history of the human homeworld. Even knowing all of this we did not have the capacity to imagine the attack that the humans threw at our world.

Bears. That's what they call them. The humans have a variety of life on their world who share a very similar evolutionary path to my race. They have multiple species that fall into the niche, the most common of which they call a "seal." In the coldest regions of their world they have a giant, mighty, and fierce predator called a "polar bear" which feeds on seals. Moving toward their equator they have various other variants of the "bear" archetype, all of which are monstrous in size and which can easily maul and consume anyone of my race. The humans attacked with bears.

They didn't send ships of bears that were armed. No. They didn't even send ships at all. They didn't even send bears. They shipped automated drones to us via a series of circuitous routes. When the drones made it through customs inspections, they simply flew away. We presumed, based on the technology, and the addressing on the exterior casing, that they were delivering themselves to their intended *recipients, thus saving us the trouble. We were right, and so very wrong all at once.*

You see, these drones each contained the working instructions to locate an area suitable for their attack. They consumed local resources to build a clone maturation facility. Then the facility used the genetic material it brought with it to start cloning these bears. Meanwhile, the drone moved on to build another facility.

It was ten cycles, and some additional days, after the humans' deadline to negotiate for our crimes when the first bear attack happened. Scientists, studying deep in the forest, recorded the entire event and streamed it in real-time as they were slaughtered by a previously-unknown-to-us giant brown predator. It was not long after that attack that attacks from a white-colored variant of the predator began

happening all along our northernmost and southernmost cities. By the time we realized something was amiss and located the first cloning installation, there had been hundreds of bear attacks. Thus far we have found 9,153 cloning facilities scattered across our lands. We have no idea how many bears they have created. We have no idea how to even begin to count them because the variant known as "polar bears" are invisible to our thermal scans and they blend in with the ice *that they traverse. Of the remaining varieties of bears, we have conducted a census that shows at least 10 MILLION specimens roaming about in our forests.*

Council, we are begging you for help, not with resolving the bears issue, but rather, to prevent the escalation of this war. When we contacted the humans to discuss the situation, they simply replied "We hope you like the bears. You must answer for your war crimes if you wish to avoid further conflict. Our escalation will include Orcas and sharks. You have been warned."

We do not know what these two animal types are, but surely, they must be far worse than the bears if they are to be the second wave. We need a neutral party to intercede on our behalf and get the humans

to stall their attacks and negotiate peace with us. Please, fellow members of the Council, we are begging for your help.

Flight Delay

Every flight starts the same. Every flight ends the same. Every flight goes the same way while in transit: bad food, smelly fellow passengers, annoying children, bad entertainment, and people spending too long on the stretch deck and/or in the bathrooms. It doesn't matter which spaceliner you take and it doesn't matter what type of vessel you're in. In fact, it's the same for intraplanetary trips, too. Travel is travel all the galaxy over.

Welcome aboard! We know you have a choice in space liners, and we're

pleased you chose to trust us with your journey.

Our flight time to Relay Hub 717 will be 43 hours, 17 minutes. Mobility time will be granted by sections during the flight so that you all have an equal opportunity to make use of the health benefits of not being strapped to your seat for the duration of our journey. Meals will be offered every 6 hours, on the hour, starting 2 hours and 7 minutes into our flight time.

Please refrain from excessive restroom use and remember that you're stuck in this ship with everyone else for the duration of the flight, so be kind and respectful of everyone!

When we arrive at Relay Hub 717, all passengers will deboard the craft so that we can cycle out the systems and recharge all life support for the next leg of this vessel's journey. Those continuing on with this vessel will be called to reboard after the 3-hour resupply time so don't wander too far inside the concourse!

Please pay attention to the flight attendants as they go through all of the safety features of this Grendarian e762 Transport Vessel. If you are seated near an EVA suit deployment closet and/or near an evacuation airlock, you will be asked to help in the event of an emergency. If you are unable, or unwilling, to assist in such an event, please let the nearest flight *attendant know so that we may swap you with another passenger who is willing and able to assist in the event of an emergency.*

Now, buckle up and enjoy the flight!

The overly cheerful Captain recited the flight preamble, and the flight attendants completed their necessary demonstrations with smiles, each with a varying level of sincerity. The various species in the passenger cabin all took their seats, with varying levels of grumpiness about the state of their luggage storage, and everyone buckled in for departure. No one noticed the singular human traveling alone among the cadre of many colors and shapes and various numbers of limbs wielded by the passengers. No one noticed because no one cared. Humans were only mildly special in that they were a new race to the heavens and still somewhat rare outside of official human transports. But, because everyone was busy and focused on their own plans, no one thought anything of the human amongst them.

The human, likewise, was focused on her journey and was pleased to have a seat that wasn't too crowded and in a place near where she found a spot for her carry-on luggage. Her portable terminal was neatly stowed under the seat in front of her, and she relaxed, closed her eyes, and began to doze.

The flight was perfectly normal and predictable and supremely boring, until the moment it wasn't.

The vessel shuddered, a ripple of concussion traversing the floor of the passenger cabin. Screams of surprised passengers being tossed around the stretching space on the upper deck careened through the vents, alerting all to the plight of the passengers above. The pressure masks deployed, dangling in front of each and every breathing orifice for those seated in the regular cabin. The drink service cart rolled into one flight attendant, knocking it forward several rows before rolling back toward the stern of the craft and crashing through a lavatory door. The lights blinked and went out. The emergency strips on the ceiling and the floor lit up.

A moment of absolute quiet stretched into an infinite pause of consciousness as everyone's minds caught up with the situation they now found themselves in, and then the screams began. Screams of fear. Screams of pain. Screams of shock and confusion. The screams lasted a greater eternity than the silence that heralded them before they, too, were broken by the sound of the ship's intercom.

"Attention passengers. We have experienced an ... incident." The pause gestated, cutting the passenger chatter as it began to start up again. "As of this moment, we are fine, with full cabin pressure and more than ample supplies to support everyone on board until the rescue craft can arrive to refresh those supplies and tow us to the Relay Hub. Please remain calm and assist the cabin staff in any way they require. I will update ever ..." the Captain's message was drowned out by the explosion that rocked the aft section of the craft, blowing an arc of debris away from the starboard engine and casting a fabulous flame show into the darkness of space as the spilled remnants of fuel and oxygen mixed and flash combusted before freezing into a rainbow of sparkling exhaust crystals.

The gravity rippled, allowing some items to float away, firmly keeping others where they were supposed to be, and compressing some to the surfaces in a grasp tighter than intended.

The flight crew tended to their injured and then traversed the craft to tend to the injured and upset passengers. Within a half hour of the initial incident the dimmed interior of the ship was quiet as various passengers slept under the influence of calming drugs or pain killers, while others cried quietly to themselves. Many had put on their pressure masks in case they were needed.

The human rose from her seat and addressed the flight crew member nearest to her "We have a problem, and we need to inform the Captain."

"What's the problem?" the crew member asked.

"Not here," the human spoke, very quietly, leading the crew member to the nearest service bay, away from the rest of the passengers, "The air circulators stopped in the explosion."

"Yes, we know, but that's not a problem. The masks are their own life support system and will be sufficient."

"You don't understand. The circulators stopped but the air is still moving."

"What? How do you know?"

"I could feel it from my seat. Do you have a match? Or a lighter?"

"A match? No. But I do have a lighter."

"May I borrow it for a moment?"

"Yes" the crew member fumbled in their pocket and withdrew a lighter.

The human marveled at the similarity to the designs of lighters from all of the worlds, and she muttered, "I guess form really does follow function," and she fiddled with it for a moment. "Ok, now I need a napkin or something that will burn and make a small amount of visible smoke."

The crew member complied "But why?"

"This is why," the human said as she lit the paper. The smoke billowed gently away from the paper for a few centimeters before drifting sharply toward the stern of the craft. "We have a breach. We're losing air."

"SMOKE!" someone yelled "I smell smoke!"

"Please, remain calm, that was me generating a small amount of heat to seal a makeshift sample container," the human yelled back. "Don't be alarmed. It's nothing to be worried about!"

"That was a quick answer" the crew member whispered.

"We couldn't afford a panic, and it was the best impromptu reason I could come up with. Now will you let me tell the Captain?"

"Yes. Let's go."

The human, and the flight attendant, moved forward through the vessel until they reached the cockpit. Two knocks, and a passcode later, the two were admitted into the tight space of flight control where the human was able to impart the horrible news to the Captain.

"I know," was the reply, "but there is nothing I can do about it, and telling the passengers will only cause a panic which will make everything worse."

"Why can't you do anything about it? Isn't there some sort of emergency kit for this situation?"

"Yes, but it was in the section that exploded, and the backup kit was in the first place that ripped apart.

We, by sheer chance, lost both our pressure leak kits in the same accident.”

“Do you know where the leak is?”

“Yes,” the Captain indicated a specific amber alert on the display screen. “It’s in the hold, below the passenger compartment. The containment bulkheads closed the rest of the troubled areas off, but this panel of the hull seems to have a small hole in it.”

“Let me go fix it.”

“With what?”

"I don't know. I'll figure something out."

"If you go down there, you'll probably die. The temperature is not maintained at the normal comfort zone of the flight cabin."

"If no one goes down there, we will all die. Let me worry about me while I am down there."

The Captain moved in a manner that the human could best-interpret as a shrug "Ok. It's your skin."

"Can you send me a readout of the systems and what is damaged and what is working?"

"I can send it to any terminal on the ship."

"Is there a terminal down there?"

"Yes."

"Send it down there. I will see what I can do."

The human descended into the underbelly of the ship through the service ladder behind the rear-most flight service area. It was rapidly apparent that everything farther aft than that service ladder was obliterated and inaccessible. She used her com as a flashlight and stumbled her way through a disheveled pile of luggage that had broken loose, searching all the while for her own suitcase, muttering, "If I have to start somewhere, I'll start with that."

After about twenty minutes of searching in the lightless bowels of the ship, her tiny beacon hit on the very suitcase she desired, and she shouted a minor victory cry. She grabbed it and headed toward the

front of the craft where the Captain said the service terminal was.

Adjacent to the service terminal, much to her pleasure, was a small cabinet of commonly needed tools and materials, not enough to patch a significant hole, but something to work with. She unpacked her bag, adding her own tools and materials to the collection available to her, and set to work.

The first order of business was to make a low-heat, low O2 smoke using an oxidation reaction that would emit visible smoke so she could see the movement of the air around the leak. This endeavor was quick and took very few of her resources. As she approached the hole, she realized she did not, and would not in the immediate future, need the smoke to determine the hole, for the air current grew constantly as she approached the hole, leading her directly to a small puncture from a micrometeorite. It was no larger than her thumb, but it was more than enough to kill them all. Running through a mental inventory of everything available to her, she concluded that nothing would work. The crack filler would blow out of such a large opening before it could set, and the larger materials were not airtight and would only slow the leak, splitting it into a thousand smaller leaks rather than one large leak. Making things much more complicated was the jagged, ripped metal around the edge of the hole where the hull had been pushed inward upon impact.

She turned from the hole and rushed back to the ladder, ascending as quickly as she could. She greeted the attendants gathered in the area with, "I need ... four bottles of water. Four bottles of water and 3 cans of any beverage. And I need 6 snack packs that are packed in the metal foil." Without waiting for a reply, she started back down the ladder, calling up to the crew, "Just drop them down to me!"

The stunned crew gathered the things she requested and dropped them down to the open hatchway. She darted off with her hoard of newly acquired supplies.

She drank the first water quickly, not wanting to waste any more of it than was absolutely necessary, and set to work cutting the length of the bottle, allowing her to flatten the plastic into a sheet of pliable material rather than being a useless cylinder. Using the soldering iron as a heat source, she began, slowly and carefully, to heat the plastic as she pushed it against the hull's inward-facing shards, allowing them to piece through the plastic in a controlled fashion that limited the gap between the seal and the offending metal. She worked her way around the hole in this manner until the majority of the leak was controlled, only allowing the slightest of air movement around the very edges. Then she used the crack-filler gel to seal that. Knowing that the plastic itself was a fragile membrane, and not durable enough to withstand any sort of tensile torsion or compression, she began to fashion a better plate out of the can material. She, deftly and precisely, cut multiple layers of the material, applying each one to the layer before with a thin coating of crack-filling gel to glue them together. As her masterpiece took shape, the shark teeth of metal that protruded inward from the wound in the ship's side vanished beneath the make shift cap that would keep the entire ship alive long enough for rescue. Then she began the tough job. She opened the terminal and scrutinized the systems that were supposed to be on the ship and the ones that still were.

The FTL cruising engine was still intact, but it lay on the other side of a decompressed portion of the lower hull and was disconnected from all power by the intervening damage. The atmospheric engines, and their control hardware were obliterated, but their power system was still intact. The adjustment thrusters had lost all their compressed propellant, making them completely useless, but their control systems were entirely functional.

The human, alone in the dark, began to rip out the wiring. All of the wiring that spanned the interior of the ship was fair game, and she made use of all of it. The thicker cabling, designed for running high amperage power, was going to be used for that very purpose, but it would be used not for airlock doors and landing gear systems, it would be used to route power from the atmospheric engines through the harsh void of the decompressed ship to the FTL cruising drive. The low amperage lines, used for signals and data, were selectively cannibalized, killing half the entertainment system, to redirect the adjustment thrusters into the FTL cruising control computer.

When she had done all she could do within the ship proper, she searched the hold, hoping there would be a mostly generic pressure suit, somewhere, that she could wear.

While it fit extremely poorly and was designed for a four-armed service worker of some sort, she did, in fact, find one. She proceeded to make use of the mid-ship airlock and continued her work on the opposing side of the bulkhead, where a single wrong step could let her fall away into oblivion, endlessly spinning away from any chance of salvation as the infinite darkness swallowed her, and then the ship, forever.

She made no missteps. Six grueling hours later, having consumed all of the plastic from the bottles, the foil from the snack wrappers, the cans, and all of the crack-filling gel, she was ready to try to reengage the power to the FTL drive.

The ship shuddered as the engine shook in its mounts before lighting up.

The tiny human sighed in her suit, stared into the vacuum of space, and said, "Not this time, you fucker, not this time. You may get me someday, but today is not that day." She saluted the nothingness as she closed the outer airlock door and started the repressurization sequence.

The flight team wrinkled their noses as she emerged from the bowels of the ship. She imagined that she must, to them, be quite fragrant after six grueling hours inside someone else's pressure suit, but she didn't care. She walked past them and went straight to the cabin.

"Captain, I have news."

"So do I. There are no ships to rescue us for a week. We can't survive that long on our supplies."

"Well, I guess, that makes my news really good news."

"Ok, what's the news."

"The hull breach was a micrometeorite. I sealed it."

"With what?"

"Two water bottles and three beverage cans, one foil wrapper, and some crack gel."

"But, that's not ..."

"Yeah, yeah, yeah. That's not the right way to do it. That's not code. That will never hold up. I've heard them all. I don't care about any of that. I care about it being sealed right now. It is sealed right now and will stay sealed for the near future while we get this boat moving again. They can scrap it at the Relay Hub, I don't care... why? Because we will be at the Relay Hub instead of suffocating here."

"We have no way to get to the Relay Hub. The slow engines are completely gone and the FTL has no power and no controls."

"Well, you're partly right. The atmo engines are completely gone. That was the big explosion. But their power supply was still there. It ain't much, but it is something."

"That doesn't help us with no engines attached to it."

"Well, I sort of went ahead and solved that problem. The FTL is attached to those power banks. The FTL doesn't need any fuel, it just uses the raw power output. The banks run the engines and the fuel pumps and, well, honestly a lot of other systems we don't need right now, so I disconnected them all and rewired the ship so that the FTL can suck those power cells dry."

"But, that's not safe!"

"You are 100% right, sir. It's not. But it's a hell of a lot safer than sitting here waiting to run out of air ... or food ... or water ... Oh, by the way, the water recycler is fried. So, we would, eventually, run out of water.

Would you rather risk an unsafe power conversion or just sit and wait to die?"

"Well."

"You actually have to think about it? It's 100% chance of death or 43% chance of the FTL melting down in the back where no one is anyway... leaving us in the same situation we were in before I made it work."

"OK. I see your point. But my FTL system is dark."

"Yeah, about that, the FTL control circuits were fried out. The atmo flight circuits were fried out."

"So how am I supposed to fly?"

"The thrusters."

"What? They're not good for anything other than the teeniest, tiniest nudges as we approach docking."

"Yep, I know. But all their compressed gas is gone so they aren't even good for that. But what they ARE good for is issuing directional commands to a flight control system."

"Wait, are you saying…"

"Yes. I slaved the FTL to the thruster controls. It won't be easy, but it should work. No autopilot for us for the rest of the trip, but if someone is actively flying, we should be able to get there … The navcomp is even still working so it can keep the person doing the active flying on course. Go ahead, try it."

The Captain engaged the thrusters and pushed on the forward adjustment joystick, and the ship lurched forward, the stars stretching into the familiar streaks of FTL cruising. The navcomp chimed in with its ever-cheerful and helpful voice to indicate that the ship was off course and presented a correction vector overlaid against the desired course and the dark void of space that lay outside the cockpit window in between the starlines.

"How did you do all of this?" The Captain asked.

"It's sort of what I do. I fix situations that are beyond all hope. I get sent to places where bad things are happening, or happened, and I fix them well enough to salvage whatever can be saved. This is the first time that I was the very thing I needed to salvage, though. I wonder if I can write this off on my taxes double."

The Captain looked dumbstruck, "This is the type of thing you do all the time?"

"Yep, sure is."

"Who do you do this work for?"

"My employer is a government contractor that works for the Earth government. Not many people have heard of them, and that's fine."

"Thank you. I'm sorry, what is your name?"

"Angela. Angela MacGyver. You can call me either Angie or Mac; I don't have a preference."

"Thank you, Angie, for saving my ship and these passengers. I wish I could offer more than words."

"You can. Get us to the Relay Hub so my work here isn't wasted." With that, she winked at the Captain and left the cockpit. She returned to her seat to the dismay of the nearby passengers' noses, and she fell asleep.

KaBOOM!

The humans welcomed us when we arrived on their world. They gave us tours of their most famous and prestigious places. We met their most famous and prestigious people. They showcased all of their architectural marvels. They showed us all of their fascinating "technology."

We marveled at their means of harnessing electricity to do their bidding in ways that we had never imagined. We marveled at the magical ingenuity needed to harness those elementals in such a way as to make rocks do their math for them. We marveled at how they managed to use brute force and raw heat to shape everything in their world to their whims.

Truly, for a species so backward in so many ways, astounding that they could achieve the greatness that they had managed to build such a world-wide travel and commerce network.

When we asked them to see the mages behind all of their astounding engineering, they showed us "tech wizards" and artificers, neither of whom showed any magical prowess at all. They merely used the tools created by the true wizards but were not the beings who imbued the tools with the elemental forces needed to work.

When we explained what we wanted to the humans, they took us to massive facilities that they called "power plants" and told us that the facilities were where the power came from to make the tools work. We tried, again, to explain that we sought the minds who enslaved the elemental energy into their tools to allow others to use the tools, not the tools themselves.

One of their kind, a lower-ranking official, claimed to understand what we needed and suggested we go to a "junior high" and see "a science project" about the basics of electricity. We went with the officials, only to discover the massive insult they were serving to us. They tried to explain that there was no magic, that they just made use of a basic force of the universe, and that the simple toys in front of them, which they used to entertain children, provided the foundational knowledge we needed to understand that they did not have any wizards who imbued their tools with the captured elementals of the magical realm to make their tools work.

We could not suffer such insolence and insulting behavior, and we left, calling for our retrieval packs to whisk us away from this "junior high" and return us to the ship we had parked in their "park." We crystalled the homeworld with the update on our situation, and they, too, thought the hubris of the humans to be unexpected and unacceptable. War was declared upon the human world for the gravest of insults they had issued to us. Clearly, their wizards numbered so few, and were such a secret, that they had to keep them hidden and safely sheltered from all others. Our tacticians estimated that, given how few wizards the humans must have, they should be easy to conquer, and then we would force them to reveal those who had harnessed all of their magical forces to shape their world. We would share our knowledge with them and make them share their knowledge with us. We would show them how to be good interstellar neighbors in the spirit of cooperation but only after they had paid for their insolence and lies. They, clearly, were an upstart and arrogant race who needed to be broken before they could join the greater community of worlds.

The war has been raging for five years. We are unable to establish a beachhead on the human world

and cannot make a telering to enable a massive ground troop invasion. Even if we were able, I am not sure it would be effective. Our soldiers are equipped with the standard of our invasion forces: each platoon assigned one combat mage, ten archers, three combat medics, fifteen spearmen, and twenty foot infantry. They are equipped with the best equipment and armor we have to offer, with the swordsmen fully covered in a mixture of titanium plates and maile, and an alloyed shield strapped to their back for when they may need it. The remainder of the platoon are outfitted in similar armor as their roles allow to protect them to the highest level possible without impairing their function. Our troops have been considered the might of the galaxy and have never faced such difficulty as we have seen in trying to invade the human world.

For the first few months, each and every landing we attempted was successful. Each ship landed cleanly and without incident at our target location, and we were met by a diplomat who requested we discuss peace and wished to understand how they had offended us so terribly that we chose to declare war. Each time we executed the diplomat. Each time the ship vanished from our crystalcom network within seconds of the execution. It took us a year to understand that the ceremonial military escort that

had accompanied the diplomat was, without exception, armed with a cohort of battle mages. The moment we unleashed our violence they unleashed theirs without restraint, reducing our ships to scrap.

We were baffled by this as our scans from high altitude had still failed to reveal to us any locus of magical forces. We could not find any nexus point that would betray the location of wizards of any sort to us, let alone a concentration of battle wizards who, surely, were training more of their kind in face of our invading fleet. The humans, it seems, were far more excellent at their stealth veils than any race we have ever encountered OR their magicians were so few that they had to preserve them in secret facilities ... or both.

After a year of failures, we began to launch covert landings in an attempt to establish a foothold on their world. We were certain, if we could complete a telering, that our mass invasion would quickly overrun their military forces and the number of battle mages we could deploy would easily overpower the responding force the humans could provide. Victory would be ours if only we could get a telering constructed.

Each landing, successfully as they were, did not yield the results we desired, but it did gather extremely powerful intelligence for us. Every confrontation with the humans went the same way: our archers would fire volley after volley, sometimes eliminating a few of their individual soldiers but never penetrating their hulking armored beasts. While the arrows were in flight our battle mage would conjure illusions or shields or even make use of the KaBOOM spell to distract the humans so that our spearmen and swordsmen could advance within range.

Then the humans, ALL OF THE HUMANS, would release hundreds, sometimes, thousands, of mini KaBOOM spells in our direction. Each one used to push a tiny projectile at us. These projectiles, flung by a KaBoom, ripped through our armor. Some of them shredded through trees and various other obstacles to wound our soldiers. Only a strong magical shield, thrown up by the battle mage, using all of their power, was enough to stop the onslaught of the little projectiles. But it was enough, at least until they unleashed the larger KaBooms. A single KaBoom released from any of the armored beasts passed through the strongest magical shield any mage was able to produce, and the mage was, quite simply, not there any longer. Those around the mage were,

inevitably, covered in gore as the mage was reduced to component pieces. The shield would fall and the rain of projectiles would resume until our soldiers were all dead or had retreated into the ship and evacuated the encounter.

Sometimes, though, evacuation by ship was not a path to safety. The humans, it seems, have harnessed air elementals not only for commerce and civilian transport but also for military purposes, and those aircraft are, also, equipped to deploy stored KaBoom spells at us. For every ten craft we landed on their world, only one would return to orbit, and it was, always, barely staffed and badly damaged.

For the past five years, we have continued in this manner, landing ships and engaging the humans, only to be shredded by their flagrant and excessive use of the KaBoom spell in strength levels varying from the tiniest, most delicate use to spells large enough to obliterate entire landing craft in one shot. For five years we have witnessed their use of the KaBoom spell propelling projectiles at use from a distance.

I am reporting to you now, though, that things have changed. Our last invasion effort sent double the force. It consisted of two motherships, each with the requisite 24 landing craft, each with the two platoons to deploy on their world. The humans broadcast a message to us demanding we cease our hostilities and leave or they would be forced to demonstrate weaponry beyond our comprehension, even greater than anything we could imagine, against one of the two motherships. Our response was for one of the ships to deploy its entire invasion fleet at once.

As the 24 landing craft descended through their atmosphere, a single, magically inert projectile was hurled from the face of their world at us using one of their KaBoom spells. The spell was long-burning, rather than the usual immediate and fierce instant explosion, and it propelled the object upward at a rate that seemed quite lazy compared to the projectiles they deployed against our ground forces. We watched from the empty mothership as it approached the full mothership. We chuckled and laughed, knowing that, at its speed, it would merely bounce off the hull of the vessel and fall back to earth, burning upon reentry into their atmosphere.

But then it happened.

The biggest KaBoom we have ever witnessed. The other mothership was no longer there, and within seconds, our ship was pelted by debris fragments,

creating massive breeches in our hull that allowed nearly half of our atmosphere to vent into space before we could close all of the pressure doors. Half of our elementals were purged from our ship, leaving only inoperable controls. About half of our landing craft returned to our ship, the remainder being destroyed before they could do anything further. Those who returned informed us that they had received a message from the humans, being broadcast on all frequencies at us. It informed them that, "That was the smallest of our nuclear missiles. It was only one. We have tens of thousands ready to be deployed should you return, and we will be launching a fleet to carry many of them to your world. You have been warned. Your surrender is expected upon our arrival. We do not wish to drop such weapons against your homeworld."

As the Captain of the surviving ship from that encounter, I must implore you. Surrender to the humans. They may only know how to use the KaBoom spell in combat, but they have mastered it beyond any levels that we can imagine. They have tolerated this war long enough and are now fed up with us. Clearly, they were toying with us this entire time, allowing us to weaken our forces before choosing to invade our world. Perhaps, if we surrender, they will have mercy upon us in a way that we did not show them. Perhaps, if we surrender, they will be satisfied with the end of the war rather than annihilating us for daring to challenge them. Perhaps they are better than we in this manner and this war is a lesson we should learn from this fledgling race, for it was our hubris that led to our current situation ...

KaBOOM!

Accompanying Artwork

For this edition of this book the artwork has been consolidated into this section rather than placed throughout the interior.

This is for formatting purposes to ensure the best artwork experience for you, the reader.

Woken Giant

The Venue

ONE NIGHT ONLY
HONEST ABE
DELIVERS !!!
THE GETTYSBURG ADDRESS
ONE NIGHT ONLY
ONE NIGHT ONLY

ONE NIGHT ONLY
DUELING ELVIS
OLD ELVIS AND YOUNG
ELVIS PRESLEY TAKE
THE STAGE TOGETHER

The Looking Glass

Accompanying Artwork

Humanity Flies

Witness

The Reality Bomb

The Park

BREAKING NEWS
USABC:
CRYPTIC
MESSAGE
FROM
SPACE!

Momentary Reflection

Accompanying Artwork

Empty

Immortality

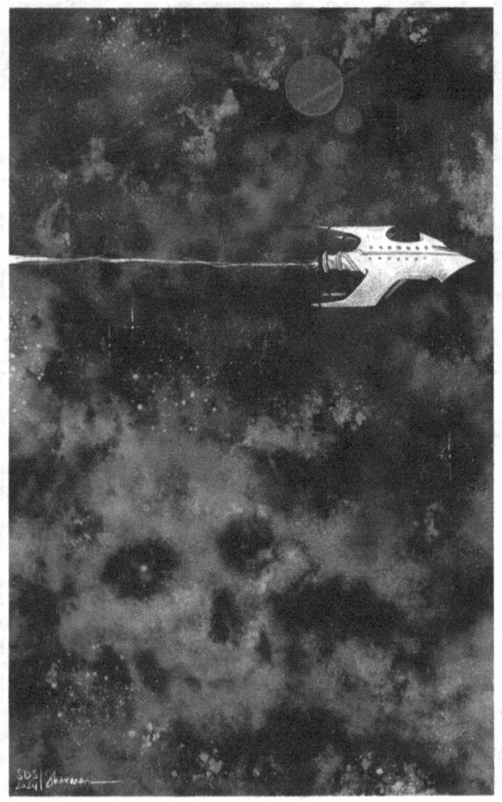

Programming Oversight

STH 2024

STH 2024

Regression

The Replacement Engineers

Bears

Flight Delay

KaBOOM!

STH 2024

STH 2024

Accompanying Artwork

Accompanying Artwork

Artwork Appendix

Artists in Alphabetical Order

Alyssa Avery

alysaavery.com

Pages: 226 & 227

Bonniejean Boettcher

bonniejeanb.com

Narrator (anticipated)

Laura Cassellius

artwanted.com/lehorning

Pages: 198, 199, 201, 202, 203, 216, & 217

Matt Haynes

narratormatt.com
Narrator

Sheldon Hussierre

Pages: 197, 204, 221, 222, 235,
236, & 237

Pavlo Kandyba

www.masterogon.art
Cover Artwork: Astral Travel

Michelle Kapschull

Cover Design

jorolero - creative

jorolero.com
Pages: 213, 214, 215, 224, 225,
229, 230, & 231

Scott Sherman
WitchRender.com
Pages: 196, 206, 207, 208, 209,
210, 211, 218, 219, 223,
232, & 233

Rory Turnbull
Page: 205

Story Notes

Woken Giant - circa 2014, I believe there is a lot more I can do with this story, so I expect another version will appear some day in the future. It has not been published anywhere else. The title is a reference to the Japanese comment about the USA after having bombed Pearl Harbor.

The Venue - previously published in October 2017 to Daily Science Fiction (now defunct).

Humanity Flies - circa 2015. Not previously published.

The Looking Glass - circa 2013. Not previously published.

Witness - circa 2011. Not previously published.

Reality Bomb - circa 2018. Not previously published.

The Park - started circa 2014; finished for this volume. Not previously published.

Momentary Reflection - inspired by the murder-suicide in a town near me in which a man killed his children and wife before killing himself. Story was written in 2014.

Empty - circa 2014. Not previously published.

Immortality - circa 2018. Not previously published.

Programming Oversight - written as a response to [WP] "Unfortunately nobody thought to program the replicators to know that antipasta is not, in fact, antimatter pasta" as posted by u/LordMlekk

Regression - written as a response to [WP] "Every time you're killed you wake up in a parallel universe that has, among other things, slightly less modern technology" as posted by u/SlowCrates

Replacement Engineers - written for [HFY]

Bears - written for [HFY]; despite the similar theme of Woken Giant, the two stories are not entangled.

Flight Delay - written for [HFY]; Yes, the name is a reference to one of my favorite childhood television programs.

KaBOOM! - written for [WP] "They only ever use a single spell in combat" "Yea but they're REALLY good at that one spell" as posted by u/EndorDerDragonKing and cross-posted in [Humans, Fuck Yeah!]

About the Author

Justin T. Cole spends far too much time sitting in front of a computer, whether it is performing his regular vocational duties, writing something, watching some video program, or fiddling with a half-dozen other projects. When he is not busy on his computer, he spends time supporting his wife and kids' artistic efforts in a variety of ways or telling one of his dogs to "move your butt" because it has chosen to lay in the exact wrong spot ... again.

Savantia and Other Stories